Disney
Tim Burton's
The Nightmare Before Christmas

Adapted by Lauren Clauss
Illustrated by Jeannette Arroyo

A GOLDEN BOOK • NEW YORK

The movie *Tim Burton's The Nightmare Before Christmas* story and characters by
Tim Burton, copyright © 1993 Disney Enterprises, Inc.

A crowd of creatures stood waiting in the center of Halloween Town. When Jack Skellington—the Pumpkin King—arrived, they cheered, celebrating another successfully spooky holiday.

"Great Halloween, everybody," Mayor said as the group quieted down.

"I believe it was our most frightful yet," Jack added. "Thank you, everyone."

But Jack soon left the party and joined his ghost dog, Zero, in the quiet graveyard. After so many Halloweens, he was growing bored with the same old things.

Sally, a rag doll created by scientist Dr. Finkelstein, watched
Jack wander through the graves. She understood how he felt.
She also wanted more in life, but Dr. Finkelstein refused to set

Jack walked all night with Zero, going deep into the woods. He came to a clearing surrounded by seven large trees, each with a different door painted on it.

"What *is* this?" Jack wondered aloud.

He was most curious about the door with a
pine tree symbol. He opened the door and was
swept up by a strong gust of wind. The wind
pulled Jack down into darkness.

Jack landed on a snowy hill above a town filled with colorful lights and joyful sounds. He was thrilled! There were so many new things for him to see, from snow falling to people singing songs to a large man shouting, *"Ho-ho-ho!"* Jack thought he heard the man being called Sandy Claws.

Jack learned that he was in a place called Christmas Town!

Jack returned to Halloween Town and told everyone about his adventure. While people were excited to hear about the unusual Sandy Claws, they didn't understand the strange, un-scary holiday Jack described.

After weeks of learning all he could about Christmas, Jack
made an announcement.

"This year, Christmas will be ours!" he shouted.

Everyone cheered—except Sally. She had picked
a weed in Jack's yard, which had grown into a
Christmas tree and then caught fire! Considering that
a bad omen, Sally expected Jack's plan to end horribly. But
because she loved him, she vowed to do her best
to help him succeed.

Preparations for Christmas were under way in Halloween Town, and everyone was pitching in! Dr. Finkelstein made skeleton reindeer, and ghosts and ghouls decorated the square. And despite her reservations, Sally sewed Jack his own Sandy Claws suit.

Jack called on Lock, Shock, and Barrel for a
top-secret job. They ran into Christmas Town and
kidnapped Sandy Claws! Jack needed Sandy Claws out of the
way so *he* could deliver presents this year.

Jack told the trio to make Sandy Claws comfortable, but
instead they took him to their boss, Oogie Boogie, a villain
who loved to cause chaos!

Soon it was Christmas Eve, and Jack was ready to spread joy.
"We're off!" he shouted to an excited crowd. With Zero
leading his coffin sleigh, Jack shot into the sky.

But the scary toys Jack delivered were not at all what the children expected. Instead of joy, Jack's presents spread fear throughout the world!

As the residents of Halloween Town watched Jack through a witches' cauldron, Sally worried that something would go wrong. She knew what she had to do.

"Where'd they take that Sandy Claws?" she shouted, and left to find him.

While Jack flew home, spotlights shone on him, and explosions went off all around.

"They're thanking us for doing such a good job," Jack told Zero. But he quickly learned they were trying to blast him out of the sky!

Jack's sleigh was damaged, and it fell to the ground, landing in a graveyard. At first Jack was disappointed—everything had gone wrong, despite his good intentions.

But then he realized that although he had wanted
to do something wonderful, he had also been trying
to be someone he was not. The realization cheered him.
He was ready to be the Pumpkin King once more!
He vowed to make next year's Halloween the best ever.
But this night wasn't done.

"Come on, Zero," Jack said, heading back to Halloween
Town. "Christmas isn't over yet!"

Back in Halloween Town, Jack raced to Oogie Boogie's lair and was shocked to find not only Sandy Claws, but also Sally. They were both tied up and in danger. Jack was touched that Sally had tried so hard to help him. Jack freed the pair—but then *he* was trapped by Oogie Boogie!

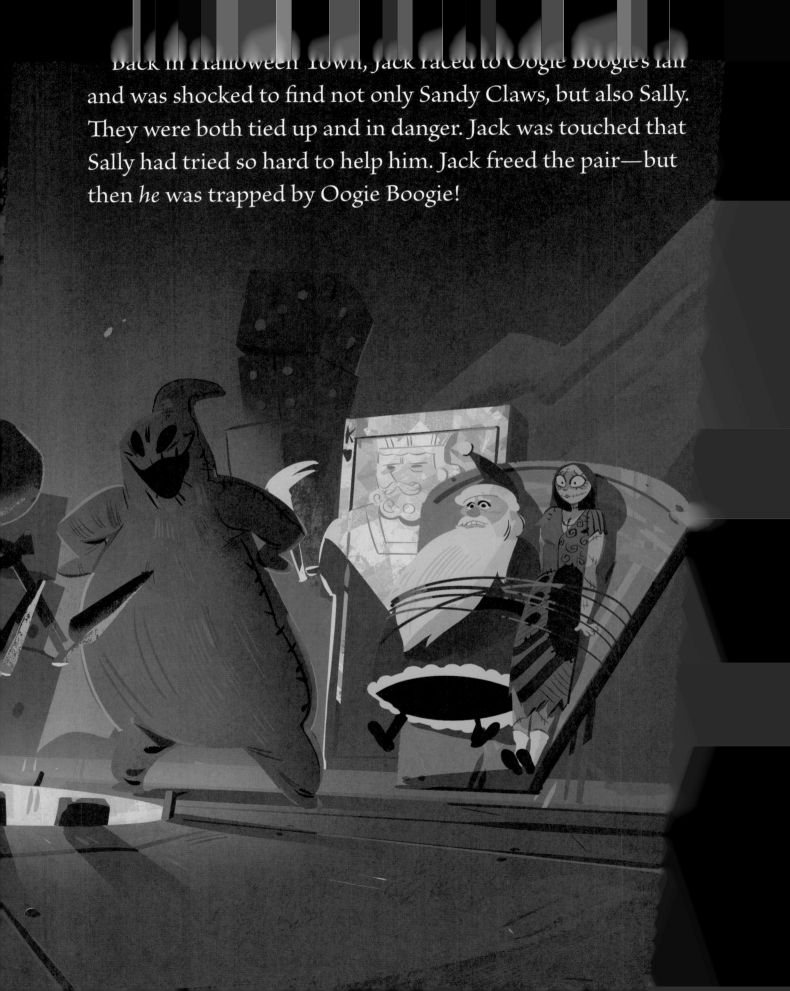

"How dare you treat my friends so shamefully!" Jack shouted. He was able to pull a loose thread on Oogie Boogie's burlap-sack body until it fell apart, and all the bugs that made up Oogie Boogie scattered everywhere!

Jack apologized to Sandy Claws for what he had done. "I hope there's still time," he said.

"To fix Christmas?" Santa Claus asked. "Of course there is! I'm Santa Claus!" And with a little magic, Santa floated away to save the holiday.

While everyone celebrated Jack's return, Santa Claus flew overhead and brought snow to Halloween Town for the first time.

Later, Jack found Sally in the graveyard and took her hands. He was happy that things were back to the way they were meant to be.